A Storybook
of Witches, Wizards and Magicians

WRITTEN BY NICOLA BAXTER
ILLUSTRATED BY KEN MORTON

ARMADILLO

This edition is published by Armadillo, an imprint of Anness Publishing Ltd,
Blaby Road, Wigston, Leicestershire LE18 4SE; info@anness.com

www.annesspublishing.com

If you like the images in this book and would like to investigate using
them for publishing, promotions or advertising, please visit our website
www.practicalpictures.com for more information.

Publisher: Joanna Lorenz
Editor: Elizabeth Young
Editorial Consultant: Ronne Randall
Designer: Amanda Hawkes
Production Designer: Amy Barton
Production Controller: Don Campaniello

PUBLISHER'S NOTE
Although the advice and information in this book are believed to be accurate and true at
the time of going to press, neither the authors nor the publisher can accept any legal
responsibility or liability for any errors or omissions that may have been made.

Manufacturer: Anness Publishing Ltd,
Blaby Road, Wigston, Leicestershire LE18 4SE, England
For Product Tracking go to: www.annesspublishing.com/tracking
Batch: 6063-20944-1127

A Storybook
of Witches,
Wizards and
Magicians

Readers, Beware!

You live in a world that is full of magic. Didn't you realize that? Well, think of it this way. Magic is what we call strange things that happen without any reason that we can see. If your cat said "Good morning!" to you when you woke up today, if your orange juice flew into the glass all by itself, if you were early for school without even trying, then you'd know that magic had been at work. But can you really explain everything else that happens to you?

Do you know why you sometimes remember your dreams — and sometimes don't? Do you know why one day everything goes right — and another it doesn't? Do you know why leaves are green but people (almost) never are?

Of course, there might be perfectly good explanations for all of these odd things and many more that you can think of. There might be. Or maybe Wilma the Witch, or Midnight the Wizard, or Mr Marvel the Magician has been at work. Who? Oh, you'll just have to read on to find out …

Contents

Which Witch?

One witch in a town is bad enough. Even if she is not a really evil witch, she will still feel the need to cast some spells from time to time. Practice, as you know, makes perfect. But until the practice is finished, those spells are not perfect. And spells that are not perfect mean trouble. Yes, one witch is bad enough. Imagine what twin witches might do!

The folks who lived in Mazewich didn't need to imagine. They knew. Helga and her twin sister Orla had been born in the town. There, when they were chubby toddlers, they had turned their first mice into frogs. It wasn't long before they were at school, turning books, bicycles and even teachers into frogs.

When they finished school – well, it would be more accurate to say that the school was finished, since it closed down due to lack of teachers – they became full-time witches in a town that by now had more than its fair share of fat, green frogs.

Now, the sisters were identical. They both had bright red hair, large noses and knobbly knees. Even their own mother couldn't tell them apart, which was very unfortunate. You see, although the sisters were alike in every other way, they were very, very different when it came to magic. In short, Orla was a clever and sensible witch. Helga was hopeless and didn't even know it, which made things worse.

Orla's turning-everything-into-frogs stage was over by the time she was fourteen. All young witches go through it. It's just a phase. But Helga was still filling the house with hoppers when she was fifty-four.

Some witches have natural talent. Some witches should give up after a week and take up scuba diving or aerial photography instead. Helga would have made an excellent wrestler, a first-class digger-driver, or a skilled sludge-spreader. She was simply the wrong kind of person for the delicate and dangerous art of magic.

For years, Orla tried to help her sister. She even dragged her twin up the Magic Mountain to meet some of the best witch experts of the age. It was no use at all. Orla gave up.

Seeing that there was nothing she could do to improve her sister's pitiful skills, the competent witch decided to set up business by herself. She moved to the other side of town and set up shop in a tree trunk on the edge of Mazewich. Folks who needed help would come to the tree and knock on the little door. Orla never let them in – she was too afraid that someone would steal her spellbook or her special collection of bat droppings – but she would climb up into the branches of the tree and talk to her visitors from on high. Her clients seemed to like the fact that they could only see part of the witch through the leaves. After all, she *was* a witch, and like all witches, she was pretty hideous. The leaves were a big improvement. In this way, clever Orla did a roaring trade.

While anyone with warts or a case of collywobbles beat a path to Orla's door, sensible townsfolk didn't go anywhere near Helga. To attract customers (even witches have to eat), she cut her prices. It didn't help. The poorest person in town would not take a problem to Helga. It wasn't worth the risk.

Helga was not a witch who had good ideas, but one morning as she brushed her hair with a handy hedgehog she had a very bad idea. She thought it over and could find no flaw in it. The same afternoon, she too set up shop in a tree trunk on the edge of Mazewich – about six yards from her sister.

You can guess what happened. To people with a pressing problem, trees all look the same. When the witch looks the same too, what is a person to do? On the first evening, an elf called Giggles disappeared forever (although a fat frog who seemed to be permanently in hysterics went to live in his little house), and a goblin called Gertrude, who had hoped for a spell to give her a beautiful singing voice, acquired a croak that could shatter drainpipes.

By the next morning, word had gone around the town. From that moment on, neither Orla nor Helga had a single customer. The people of Mazewich may be silly, but they're not totally mad.

High above the ground, the twins met on a handy branch.

"This is a fine thing," said Orla. "Now neither of us has any customers."

"Well, I didn't have any before," said Helga. "I don't know why."

Orla yelped. It wasn't fury at her sister, although that would have been understandable. A large hornet had just stung her on the nose. Orla's nose was not attractive at the best of times, so the redness and swelling made very little difference. But it *hurt*.

"These horrible hornets have been bothering me all day," moaned the witch. "If only someone would get rid of them."

Before she could utter another word, Helga was hopping down from the tree and adding to the frog population once again.

There were — and there still are — an enormous number of hornets in and around Mazewich. Enough, at any rate, to keep Helga happily employed for years. She feels useful. Orla can get on with her sensible spells in peace. And if some of the local frogs have started to fly, that can't really matter, can it?

Wilma, the Wandering Witch

When a witch starts to wander, you have to look out. You see, a witch who is always on the move is never around when you need her. More to the point, she is never around when one of her own spells goes wrong and needs to be fixed. A wandering witch, like Wilma, can leave a trail of devastation behind her that makes a hurricane look like a gentle breeze.

Wilma didn't mean to cause problems. She did her best to help people and she was quite a clever witch, but she was careless. She often acted first and thought about what she was doing later.

To be fair, it isn't always a witch's fault when things go wrong. People who come to ask for help from witches are often not very clear about what they really need. Take Mrs Blibble, for example. This old elf woman had had painful feet for ages. Her friends were constantly urging her to stop moaning and get something done about them. They meant that Mrs Blibble should go to the doctor in the nearby town. But the old elf didn't really like doctors, so she went to Wilma instead.

"I can't go on any longer," she told the witch, "with these painful feet. Can you make them better?"

Wilma nodded. She didn't stop to find out *why* Mrs Blibble's feet hurt her, she simply waved her arms in the air and said a few toe-twisting words.

"It won't work immediately," she said. "You need to go home and go to bed. In the morning, your feet will feel fine."

Now, the real reason for Mrs Blibble's tender toes was that her shoes were too tight. Mr Miggen the cobbler could have solved the problem in ten minutes. Wilma solved the problem in quite another way. When Mrs Blibble woke up the next morning, she had very comfy feet – for a duck! But when she waddled over to Wilma's to complain, she found that the witch was long gone.

Problems like this happened everywhere that Wilma went. All over Elfland, there were dogs who walked backwards, cows who gave spinach juice instead of milk, doors that wouldn't shut and mothers with babies who could speak sixteen languages but couldn't be understood by anyone. All of these were Wilma's work.

This might have gone on for many more years if Wilma had not made a fatal mistake. One day, she met an elf who wanted a love potion to make the girl of his choice fall into his arms. Wilma obliged, without asking any kind of sensible questions about the match. Naturally, she moved on at once.

But back in the little village of Stoneyhope, trouble was brewing. The spell had worked – oh, yes – but the girl in question was the daughter of a very powerful wizard. Wizard Weirdstone was horrified when he discovered that his daughter had run off with an elf with no common-sense and less money. He set out at once to find out how this disaster had happened. It wasn't long before he was hot on the trail of Wilma the witch.

Now Wilma was not easy to track down, so by the time he caught up with her, Wizard Weirdstone was tired and very cross. He drew himself up to his full height and bopped her on the head with his wizard's staff.

"*Ow!*" cried Wilma.

"*Wix wax wex,
Retrace your steps!*"
cried Wizard Weirdstone.

And that is exactly what the spell forced Wilma to do. She is going back over the journeys she has made, revisiting each of the places where she has caused trouble.

So, if you have a cat that barks or a chicken that loves to swim, you can be sure that one day soon, Wilma will be back. Of course, whether that is a good thing or a bad thing, only time will tell …

19

Up, Up and Away!

Zelda was a witch with a deep, dark secret. Surely, you may be saying, all witches have deep, dark secrets? Yes, but Zelda's was deeper and darker than any ordinary witchy secret. It was something that she was deeply ashamed of. It was something she hid even from her own black cat. It was certainly not something that she gossiped about with her cronies in the coven.

This is what Zelda's secret was. I will have to whisper:

She couldn't ride a broomstick!

I know, it's something all witches can do. Of course, in this day and age, many prefer to zoom about the skies on vacuum cleaners or magic mops. It made no difference to Zelda. She couldn't get airborne no matter what she did.

Now Zelda had managed to hide her unfortunate problem for most of her life. No witch *has* to use a broomstick. These days, it is usually only at ceremonies or big witch conventions that broomsticks are displayed. Then witches love to show off, doing aerial acrobatics and dive-bombing unsuspecting goblins going peacefully about their business on the ground.

Zelda steered clear of any big gathering of witches for reasons you can guess. She always politely declined when her annual invitation to the Pointed Hat Party arrived by toad.

But the older Zelda got, the more uncomfortable she felt about her failure to drive a sky-scooter. Apart from anything else, she now had baby witches of her own, and the time was fast approaching when she should teach them their first faltering flutterings on baby brooms.

Zelda decided it was time to face her fears. She left her babies with a wee-witch-watcher for the afternoon and set off into the hills with a secondhand broomstick and a large instruction manual called *New Tricks for Old(ish) Witches*.

Perched on a rock on a lonely hillside, Zelda consulted the book. She was relieved to find that it was not written in technical terms. There was no talk of angles of elevation or wind speed. Instead, the book gave common-sense instructions and encouragement.

"First straddle your broomstick," read Zelda out loud. "Do not attempt a sidesaddle position. That is strictly for experts."

Zelda hitched up her skirts and straddled.

"Now imagine that your feet are lighter than air," said the book. "You will find that they begin to float."

They did! It was not an elegant posture that Zelda found herself in, but it was progress of a kind.

"Now imagine the same lightness about the rest of you," the book went on. "Less than willowy witches may need to shut their eyes."

Zelda was not fat, but she shut one eye to be on the safe side. Then she imagined being very, very light. Up, up and away went Zelda.

"I can do it!" she screeched, frightening the feathers out of a passing pigeon.

But when Zelda looked down, she saw that the broomstick was still lying on the rock. She panicked. A frog minding its own business far below narrowly missed being flattened by a falling witch.

Zelda sat on the ground for some time, recovering from the shock and the disappointment. She knew what she had done wrong, of course. She had let go of the broomstick at just the wrong moment.

Looking back, she had always had a problem doing more than one thing at once. Several times in the last few months, she had to rescue her babies from her cauldron after trying to stir and soothe at the same time.

Zelda worked hard for the rest of the afternoon, but it was no use. She could not remember to float and hold on at the same time. The dejected witch trudged home to her family as the sun was setting.

The wee-witch-watcher looked up impatiently as she arrived.

"They've been fine," she said. "Berta ate a spider and Nora poured her spruce juice over her head. But I've got to rush. My broomstick is at the service station – the steering needs attention – and I can't go away for the weekend if I don't pick it up tonight.

The mention of broomsticks made Zelda wince. She waved off her friend and started saying a supper-spell. Then, all of a sudden, it struck Zelda that she was being a dimwitch. Why bother with a broomstick if you don't need one? Most witches *have* to use a flying machine. They can't manage without one. Zelda had proved that she could take to the air all by herself!

You will not be surprised to learn that Zelda hasn't turned down an invitation since. And other witches turn a perfectly gruesome green when Zelda shows off her stickless stunts.

The Forgetful Wizard

Once upon a time there was a very clever wizard. He knew all the spells in the Advanced Spells Book, Part 79, and he was always ready to help anyone who came to him. Unfortunately, nobody did. You see, everybody knew that the wizard was dreadfully forgetful.

It wasn't just that he forgot birthdays and shopping lists. Anyone can do that. The problem was that he was quite capable of getting halfway through a spell and completely forgetting what he was trying to do. Poor Mrs Kennykins, looking for a spell to make her laundry whiter, went home with a blue face! Little Sally Simpkins, who asked the wizard to find her lost mouse, is still looking for that mouse but has found fourteen rabbits, three cats and a kangaroo.

Well, people soon decided that visiting the wizard was just too risky. Most of them put up with their familiar old problems. They preferred the problems they knew to some completely new and much more worrying disaster. It was understandable, really.

But the wizard, whose name was Midnight, became very lonely and sad. After a wizard has finished his training, which can take hundreds of years, he looks forward to being able to use his magic for more than preparing his own breakfast. Midnight's skills were sadly underused. He still read all the wizard magazines to keep himself up to date, but no one ever trudged up the steep mountain path to his home. Weeds and wildflowers grew over the steps to his door. His cottage became as sad and neglected as he was himself. *Home Maintenance for Wizards* grew dusty on his shelf.

29

Things might have gone on in this way forever if it hadn't been for the dragon. Out of the blue one fine spring day, the dragon who lived in a nearby mountain woke up. He felt a little hungry after seven hundred years of sleep, so he strolled out of his cave and looked for something to eat. Luckily, the first thing he saw was a meadow full of fat woolly sheep. It wasn't lucky for the sheep, of course, but it was very lucky for the shepherd, his wife and his eleven children who lived nearby. Dragons are not very choosy when it comes to meals.

After enjoying a very large lunch, the dragon was too full to move. He went to sleep right there on the grass.

"He'll probably be asleep for a week or two," said the wisest villagers, "but then what will happen? Whatever are we going to do?"

For five whole days they argued and worried. They could think of nothing sensible that would save them from the dragon. Hundreds of years ago, dragons would sometimes restrict themselves to beautiful young maidens when they were hungry, but modern dragons had, the older villagers said, lost all sense of decency. Unless the villagers could think of something, they were doomed.

"We need a wizard," said a small boy.

"We *have* a wizard," replied his grandmother thoughtfully. "I wonder if he has improved at all."

"Even if he hasn't, we have no other choice," said the shepherd's wife. "Let's go and see him."

The entire village trooped its way up the path to Midnight's home. They had to hack their way through the undergrowth and cut down a few small trees, but they reached his door at last. Midnight, like the dragon, was asleep after lunch. When he awoke, he was so surprised to see so many people that at first he thought he must be dreaming. The villagers soon set him straight about *that*.

"We've got a dragon problem," they said, "and we need you to solve it."

Midnight was thrilled to be consulted again at last. He knew all about modern dragons and their dreadful ways. He spoke up at once.

"You need to make him drink a sleeping potion," he said. "Then he will sleep for another seven hundred years. There was something very like this in my last copy of *Wizard's Weekly*. Now, where did I put it?"

For two days, the wizard brewed and boiled. He pounded with his pestle and stirred with his special spoon. Each morning, villagers came running up the path to warn him that the dragon was stirring a bit more. He was clearly about to wake up.

On the third morning, Midnight was bursting with pride. He gestured grandly towards a large cauldron of some bright pink bubbly stuff.

"There it is," he said. "All you have to do is to put this in front of the dragon. He's sure to be thirsty when he wakes up. If he drinks this, he won't be awake for long."

The villagers were delighted but a little doubtful. However, when a little bird perched on the edge, took a sip and immediately started snoring, they were convinced. All they had to do now was to get the stuff down the hillside and into the meadow with the dragon.

It took another two days for the task to be completed. There were lots of volunteers for carrying heavy barrels all the way down the path to the village. The following day, when it was time to carry the barrels to the meadow, everyone felt mysteriously under the weather. No one was well enough, it seemed, to venture any nearer the dragon.

"It's probably the fumes from the potion," said the shepherd, gazing carelessly at the clouds. "Maybe the wizard can help."

Once again, Midnight was delighted to be of assistance. The barrels were loaded on to a cart, and the wizard drove the steadiest horse in the village up to the meadow. Once there, he unhitched the horse and rode it back to the village.

"You'll be all right now," he told the villagers.

"Time will tell," said the shepherd's wife darkly.

Midnight felt a little underwhelmed by the villagers'
gratitude, but he hurried back to his home feeling pretty
hopeful. It is hot, thirsty work dealing with dragons. The heat
from their flame-breathing nostrils is intense, even when they
are asleep and only flickering. Midnight was a good wizard,
but he was just as forgetful as ever. In search of a cool drink,
he slurped the first thing he found – a small cup of pink
bubbling liquid left over from the main batch.

Meanwhile, down in the valley, everything happened just as he had planned. The dragon woke, felt as dry as a desert in a drought, and eagerly guzzled the barrels of pink potion. Then, feeling rather sleepy, he slunk back to his cave in the mountain. It rumbled and smoked as the dragon snored, which the villagers felt was a very good sign.

Midnight's good name was restored. Next morning, most of the village trooped up to his door to consult him about everything from ingrown toenails to cooking disasters. You can guess what they found.

36

"I knew it – he *is* hopeless," said the shepherd's wife, who could see at once what had happened. "What good is a wizard who sleeps all the time?"

Her husband was wiser and kinder. "We haven't needed him for the last forty years," he said, "so I'm sure we'll manage without him for the next seven hundred or so. He will wake up again just before the dragon does, when he can be most use of all. And I think a famous sleeping wizard could be quite a tourist attraction!"

He was right! These days there are crowds in the village and lots of shops selling pink bubbly stuff, although they advise you to put it in your bath rather than drink it. Meanwhile, dear old Midnight is having very happy dreams. What a pity that when he wakes up at last, he will almost certainly forget them!

Wizard
Bubble Bath
Special Offer!

37

What's Wrong at Wizard School?

That is a very good question. I don't suppose you have ever visited a school for young wizards. On the whole, it's probably better to avoid it if you can. You see, just as you occasionally make a mistake with your numbers or spell something wrong, wizards don't always get things right when they are learning. And a mistake in a wizard's spelling … well, you can imagine.

When Millie Mumbleton dropped in at Wizard School one day, she realized at once that something was wrong. Young wizards were going to lessons and playing in the school yard. Some were being incredibly noisy. Others were sitting with their noses in books of magic. Every class has one or two like that. A few frazzled teachers were keeping an eye on the youngsters in the school yard. When the bell rang, all the pupils eventually went inside, after a lot of shouting at the slowest ones.

Now, you may wonder what is so strange about this. And the answer is that it isn't strange. It's just what you would expect in any school on any day of the week. But Wizard School isn't just any school. Something is badly wrong when nothing *seems* badly wrong.

Millie Mumbleton hurried straight to the headmaster's office and found him writing reports. "How can I help you?" he asked, peering over his beard at her.

Millie explained her fears. She had six young wizards of her own at the school. She knew that all was not as it should be. She was worried.

The headmaster laughed. "Everything is fine, my dear!" he said. "Please don't be concerned."

Now Millie knew for sure that something awful was going on. The last time the headmaster had spoken to her he had called her an interfering noodlepoop with no more sense than a poodle. Ancient wizards are often extremely rude. This one had never been polite to a child's parent in his life.

Millie Mumbleton left the headmaster's office and thought hard about what to do. It was clear that the school was under some kind of spell itself. She clenched her fists, her teeth and anything else that could be clenched and set off for Wizard Wootle's cave. He was the best wizard she knew – and the nastiest.

"What are you doing here disturbing me, you frog-faced woman?" asked Wizard Wootle in his usual charming way.

Millie Mumbleton explained.

"Ridiculous, you whey-faced whiny-wailer," cried the wizard. But Millie noticed that he was pushing up his sleeves as he said it. She hurried back to the school to await developments.

Pretty soon, pacing down the road with a huge tome under his arm came Wizard Wootle. He stood in the middle of the school yard and drew a circle around himself with chalk. Then he began to recite from the book. It sounded very much to Millie as if he was reading out a recipe for walnut fudge, but she had long ago realized that it was no use questioning the ways of working wizards.

"Boil it briskly until the mixture coats the spoon," intoned Wizard Wootle. "Cabramagaberdine *Splat!*" The next moment the school seemed to erupt into mayhem.

Two boys with the heads of penguins dashed past, mooing.
Green smoke enveloped the science buildings. A flock of
swans suddenly settled in the middle of the school yard and
began to dance. Just above Millie Mumbleton's head, a little
cloud appeared and began to soak her to the skin.

"Are you still here,
doodle-brain?" shouted
the headmaster, emerging
from his study.

Millie gave a sigh of relief.
Wizard School was just as it
should be again. Weird!

The Tiny, Tiny Wizard

Once upon a time, there was an elf king who had need of a wizard. His daughter, once a happy, lively child, fond of practical jokes, had became a mean and moody young woman, who sat in a corner and scowled most of the day. Everyone agreed that she must have been bewitched. Some evil magic spell had been cast over her.

"But what can I do about *that*?" groaned the king.

"We need a wizard to undo the spell," advised his wife.

A proclamation was sent out, reaching the furthest corners of the kingdom. Any wizard with spell-reversal skills was asked to come along to the elf palace at once.

A week later, three very different figures turned up at the palace gates. There was a tall, thin wizard with a flowing green beard and long robes. There was a short, plump wizard with a big book of magic and a black cat. And there was a young elf in ragged clothes.

The king looked them up and down.

"*You're* not a wizard!" he said to the elf. "You're an elf like me – well, not like me, of course. Be gone at once!"

The elf stood his ground and held out his hand.

"Of course, I'm not a wizard," he said, "but I am a wizard's helper. He is so very, very tiny that he has to be carried around. But he is the most powerful wizard in all of the nine kingdoms. Here he is, look!"

The king peered at the lad's open hand. He couldn't see a thing, but he was afraid of looking like a fool in front of the other two wizards.

"Hmmmm," he said. "Very well, come into the palace, all of you. You will each have half an hour with my daughter – I will be present, of course – to find out what is wrong and put it right. You, sir, can go first."

The tall wizard swept into the palace with an air of authority. He asked the princess questions (which she grunted at). He said a few magic words (which she frowned at). Finally, he waved his long arms and made a puff of green smoke appear around her head (which she coughed at).

"My work is done," said the tall wizard. "She is completely cured."

The king looked at his daughter. She seemed exactly the same to him – just as grumpy and unpleasant as usual.

"I think," said the king, "that it would be good to have a second opinion."

In came the plump wizard. This time there were no questions. The wizard stared hard at his patient – and she stared back. The cat did a lot of staring, too. Finally, the wizard looked in his book and found a suitable spell. He said it forwards and he said it backwards. Then he clapped his hands loudly.

"You shouldn't have any more problems," he said. "Shall I wait outside for my reward?"

48

The king shook his head. He couldn't see any change in his daughter at all. Sending the plump wizard away, he called for the tiny, tiny wizard to be brought forward.

As soon as the young elf entered the room, the princess looked a little brighter.

"I have to talk on behalf of the wizard," the young man explained. "His voice is so tiny that only someone who has been properly trained, like me, can hear it. But I must have absolute silence. Even the sound of another person's breathing can cause problems. Could I ask you, Your Majesty, to sit at the other end of this magnificent room?"

It seemed a reasonable request. The king retired to his throne, while the princess and the young elf went to a window seat far away. Even from where he sat, the king could see that *some* kind of magic was working. The princess smiled. She chatted. She even, once or twice, began to laugh. At the end of the half hour, when the king went to see what was happening, her eyes were bright, her cheeks were flushed, and she looked like an entirely different girl.

The king was delighted. "How can I ever repay your master?" he asked the young elf. The princess giggled and whispered in her father's ear.

"Certainly not!" cried the king, but his voice was not as stern as usual. "I will find this young man a job in the palace, if his master really has to leave as you say."

So the young man was given some new clothes and some work to do, at which he became very skilled. Every day, the princess whispered in her father's ear, until "Certainly not!" became

"Not until you are much older!" and then "We'll talk about it again next week!" and, at last, "Very well! The wedding can be next month!"

You have never seen a happier couple than the young elf and his royal bride. Her scowling days and his begging days were over forever. And as for the tiny, tiny wizard, no one has seen him from that day to this. But then, no one actually saw him before either, did they?

The Mixed-up Magician

Mr Marvel was a magician. Better than that, he was a *good* magician. Perhaps I should explain that in the world of elves and goblins there are three kinds of makers of magic. Witches and wizards do what they think of as important magic. They can make things better or they can make things worse – it depends how good they are at magic and what kind of mood they are in.

Magicians, on the other hand, don't ever try to cure warts or brew love potions. They are entertainers. Their only aim is to make people happy by doing tricks. That doesn't mean that they don't use real magic. Oh no. But wizards and witches, I'm afraid, tend to look down on magicians. Some other people are just as silly.

Mr Marvel's parents wanted their only son to be a wizard. Mrs Marvel looked forward to the day when she could introduce her friends to "my son the wizard" at parties. Mr Marvel hoped his son might one day be able to help him grow prize-winning peaches.

Both of them were disappointed. You see, you have to pass a lot of exams to be a wizard. It would be dangerous if just anyone could put on a pointy hat and long cloak. You don't actually have to be very clever to pass the exams, but you do have to have a good memory. That's where Mr Marvel had problems. He never could remember even the easiest spells. He would get mixed-up. And a mixed-up wizard, as you already know, is a dangerous person to have around.

A mixed-up magician is much more fun. Mr Marvel loved his job. When he was entertaining elfin children at a party, it didn't matter if the rabbit in his hat turned out to be a koala or a crocodile. That just made the children laugh. When Mr Marvel waved his wand and said, "*Sibbly bibbly, make a pudding that's jibbly!*" when he meant something else entirely, no one minded. A jibbly pudding is just as delicious.

Yes, Mr Marvel loved his job. He would have been a perfectly happy magician if only his parents had been proud of him.

"When are you going to get a proper job, Marvin?" his mother would ask, sighing over her knitting.

"I've got peach blight again," his father would groan. "It's a pity *someone* can't do something about it."

Marvin Marvel had no answer for them.

Then, one dreadful day, a wizard who should have known better made a mistake when saying a spell. He was trying to rid his garden of lots of tiny pests. He was a wizard, in fact, that Mr Marvel's father would have welcomed with open arms. But he was a careless wizard. He said his spell. He waved his arms. He made orange smoke appear all over the town. And when the orange smoke disappeared, every single toy in the town went with it.

At once, a wailing went up, as dozens of elfin children sobbed for their missing teddy bears and toy trucks. Cuddles didn't help. Chocolate cake didn't help. They cried and cried.

The wizard, for all his exams and certificates, panicked and took himself on a short holiday until the fuss had died down. The toymakers shook their heads and said that it would be at least a month before they could supply the demand. Only Mr Marvel didn't hesitate. He appointed himself Chief Entertainer of Toyless Tots that very day and the sobbing stopped within seconds.

None of Mr Marvel's tricks went right. They never did. He filled a swimming pool with custard and made the town clock strike twenty-six, but the children loved it. Grown-up elves were even more grateful. They awarded Mr Marvel a Medal of Magic – something that most wizards never achieve.

But best of all, the parents of one little boy who wasn't a little boy any more were proud as well.

"Meet my son the medal winner," said old Mrs Marvel at parties.

And Mr Marvel's father stopped complaining and bought himself a book instead. It was called *Peaches Without Pests: a prize-winner's guide* and it did the job a *lot* better than any wizard!

Mr Magic's Moving Day

For twenty years, Mr Magic the magician had lived in an old house on Abracadabra Street. It suited him down to the ground. There was a tall turret on one corner, where Mr Magic kept his doves. In the large, overgrown garden, Mr Magic's white rabbits could hop happily from dawn to dusk. Better still, in an enormous chamber that had once been a ballroom, Mr Magic could give shows to the local elves and goblins. It was a perfect house.

You can imagine, then, how upset Mr Magic was to receive a letter one morning telling him he must leave his beloved home. It seemed that the Grand Council of Wizards had decided that they needed it for a meeting hall. Wizards are fond of meetings. In fact, they are fond of any chance to show off to each other.

As a mere magician, Mr Magic had always looked up to wizards, but now he wished they would all disappear … *piff! paff! poof!* … into their pointy hats. What right had they, he wondered, to move him from the house he had lived in for so long? For the first time in his life, Mr Magic felt rebellion rising in his heart.

Like many magicians, Mr Magic had many of his best ideas in the bathtub. It took him a whole week of wallowing in bubbles to invent a plan to defeat the wizards. A few days earlier, he would have been astonished to think that he would ever be bold enough to challenge such powerful people. Now, with something so dear to him under threat, he felt he could face anything.

As he lay in his bathtub each night, Mr Magic made notes as he thought of things. Most of these got so wet that it was impossible to read them the next day. But one note was all too clear. It had just one word – witches!

Now, just as he had always respected wizards, Mr Magic had kept out of the way of witches. To his mind, they were just as clever and dangerous as wizards, but harder to understand. Mr Magic, who was afraid of heights, had never seen the point of all that whizzing about on a broomstick, for one thing. But he needed powerful magic to win his present battle, so he had to find all the help he could get.

Mr Magic approached the house of Sheba Shriveltoes, the most powerful witch in town, with trembling knees. He had never met Sheba and wondered if she would look as horrible as the stories that were told about her. In fact, for a witch, Sheba was quite good-looking. She was still hideous to human eyes, but Mr Magic found himself warming to a witch who sat in front of the fire munching cinnamon buns and reading cowboy stories.

"Ah, Mr Magic," said Sheba, which was a little startling, as the the magician had not introduced himself. "How can I help you?"

Mr Magic explained his mission. He tried to make it sound like a very small request, but Sheba was not easily fooled.

"You're asking a lot, Mr Magic," she said, "but I must confess I always like the chance to annoy the wizards. They're much too high and mighty for my liking. Now, tell me more."

When Mr Magic had explained in detail what he wanted to do, Sheba laughed. "The first thing to do," she said, "is to make sure the paperwork is absolutely watertight. Wizards are whizzes at contracts and the like. I'll get Wilma on to it. She had some legal training when she was young."

A week later, Mr Magic found himself in a room with three wily wizards. He was signing away the place on Abracadabra Street that he knew so well.

"We're not unreasonable wizards," said the one with a long orange beard. "We realize that you will need somewhere to live. I think we have found you just the place, up on Magic Mountain. Rather a good address, don't you think? Mr Magic of Magic Mountain. You can build a fine house there."

"Yes, indeed," agreed Mr Magic.

He read the contract very carefully and signed with green ink, which is the wizard way.

Mr Magic had a week left on Abracadabra Street. He could not help feeling sad as he strolled along the street, looking at the familiar trees and houses. Very soon, he would no longer be here. Although Mr Magic had made his plans, he still wished that everything could be the same as it had been for the last twenty years.

Moving day came at last. Like most magicians, Mr Magic used a spell to move his possessions. With an *ifflefifflefoop!* his chairs and chests, beds and brooms went flying on their way. When the last piece of furniture had left the house, Mr Magic leaned out of a window. Coming nearer and nearer was a loud rumbling sound. It came from a huge magic carpet, flown by none other than Sheba Shriveltoes.

And that is how Mr Magic moved away. Sheba said a few
words and suddenly, there was the house, perched on the
carpet and ready to go.

"Steering's a bit tricky," called Sheba, "but we're
off to Magic Mountain. Climb on!"

"Thanks," laughed Mr Magic, "but
I think I'll walk. See you there!"

Now Mr Magic loves his new home
as much as his old one – well, after
all, it *is* his old one! The wizards
were furious, but then, as Wilma
says, they should have read the
small print. Mr Magic gave up
his address, not his home.
And his new address, as the
wizard said, is excellent!

A Hat Without a Rabbit

Charles Chubble was the oldest pupil in the final year of Magician School. He took a lot of notes, always sat near the front, and tried not to notice that he was at least thirty years older than his classmates. Most elfin magicians decide on their career at an early age. Some say they hear a spooky voice calling them to the job. Others are attracted by the long holidays and public acclaim.

Charles Chubble didn't hear a spooky voice in his childhood, or if he did, it was telling him to be an accountant. For twenty years, Charles worked for the well-established firm of Foxworthy, Dribble and Foxworthy. He was perfectly happy and unbelievably boring.

Then, one fine morning, Charles heard a spooky voice telling him to become a magician. He never realized that it was the man next door talking on the telephone, and that anything heard through bricks and two layers of wallpaper is sure to sound a little spooky.

Charles realized all of a sudden that he was ready for a change. He made his preparations as he did everything – slowly, methodically and … it must be said … boringly. At the beginning of the new term, he was sitting with shiny shoes and a pile of brand-new notebooks in a class full of fifteen-year-olds.

The budding magician was an excellent pupil. He was top of his class in Trickonometry, Spellography and Magickry. But in Showmanship, he failed utterly.

Most magicians, when they produce a rabbit from a hat, do so with a flourish. They wave their wands, say a few magic words, close their eyes, mutter and, with a roll of drums, produce the bouncing bunny in triumph.

Charles Chubble didn't do that. He said, "Now I'm going to pull a rabbit out of this hat." And he did. It was impressive. It almost had a kind of understated charm. But it wasn't entertainment.

Charles's teachers did their best. They suggested that he might like to exchange his suit and tie for a costume with some mysterious symbols and a smattering of sequins. Charles shuddered. The teachers tried to show Charles how to make dramatic gestures on stage. His attempts were painful to watch. Think about the most embarrassing dancing your father has ever done and you come close to the awkwardness of Charles's gruesome gestures.

"I don't think you're cut out to be a performer," one of the teachers told Charles one day. "Have you considered becoming a teacher? Or perhaps doing research into the history of magic?"

But Charles was determined. "I want to be a proper magician," he said. So that was that.

Despite his failures in the Showmanship course, Charles Chubble graduated with great distinction. He immediately went out and bought himself a full magician's peformance kit, the luxury version. With the kit came a golden top hat, a tape with audience applause (in case there wasn't any) and a real, live white rabbit – who talked.

"Hi there!" said the white rabbit. "I'm ready when you are!" She was terribly eager to perform. She was delighted to hear that Charles's first show was that afternoon.

Now, no self-respecting rabbit, ready to make her big entrance on the stage, likes to hear, "I'm going to produce a rabbit," as her introduction.

"Build me up! Build me up!" she hissed to Charles from her hiding place in the hat. But Charles was moving swiftly on.

"Here it is!" he cried, with no note of surprise in his voice, and he yanked the poor rabbit out of the hat by her ears. There was polite applause, and the audience filed out. That's not a good sign five minutes into your act.

The rabbit endured another couple of performances before taking a hand (or rather, a paw) in the proceedings. She wrote out for Charles an introduction that went something like this:

"And now, straight from the wilds of outer Bolivia, it is my pleasure, no, my privilege to introduce an animal who has played before the crowned heads of Europe. Ladies and gentlemen, you are about to meet Princess Soraya, Rabbit of Destiny!"

Princess Soraya proved to be a great success, especially after Charles had bought her the exotic costume she suggested. It wasn't long before the rabbit was assisting Charles in all his tricks, adding what she called a little *pizazz* to the performance. Indeed, the day came when the rabbit was adding so much *pizazz* that the magician was hardly needed at all.

Princess Soraya decided it was time to have a quiet chat with Charles Chubble.

"Let's face it," she said. "You don't enjoy the performing and, well, let's just say that your talents lie elsewhere. We're getting more work than we can handle now. What I really need isn't a magician to perform with me, it's an agent. You know, someone to take the bookings … and the money! You'd be good at that!"

Charles thought about it. It was true that he wasn't feeling as comfortable in his new role as he had hoped. And he did like to see a pile of neat paperwork.

"We'll try it," he said, "as long as I can still wear the gold top hat."

"No problem," said Princess Soraya. "I won't be jumping out of it any more, after all. Now, about this booking in Budapest …"

The fame of the extraordinary rabbit spread far and wide. The fame of Charles Chubble, magician, faded gently into the background. He found that he was was happier taking a backstage role, and if Princess Soraya's tantrums were sometimes a little wearing, well, you have to make allowances for artistic temperament.

One day, catching sight of himself in a mirror, Charles was surprised to see that he looked distinctly like an accountant. He smiled. It felt right somehow. And there are plenty of uses for a gold top hat.

Too Much Magic!

When the mightiest wizards in Elfland decided to give a party to celebrate a thousand years of enchantment, there was a lot of bad feeling among other makers of magic in Elfland.

"Everyone knows that the very first magic was done by Wigga the Witch," muttered the ladies in pointy hats. "It's a disgrace to have a celebration without inviting the witches."

"Wizards and witches are all very well," complained the magicians, "but most ordinary folk never come across one. It's magicians who keep the spirit of magic alive among the masses."

As the date of the party drew near, the grumbling and grouching grew. The wizards found annoying little things going wrong with their plans – desserts wouldn't set, streamers wouldn't stream, and cakes collapsed alarmingly often.

"It's those witches," complained Wizard Hoo. "Of course, their magic is a puny thing compared to ours, but they are good at exasperating little spells like this."

"I wouldn't be surprised if the magicians didn't have something to do with it as well," muttered Wizard Wheeze. "They're looking suspiciously cheerful these days."

The Grand Council of Wizards held an emergency meeting.

"There's only one way to stop this party from becoming a fiasco," said the High-Hat Wizard. "We're going to have to invite the magical masses. And because no one is going to want to serve anyone else, we'll ask some ordinary elves to do the clearing up and so on."

Once they had been invited, the witches and the magicians really entered into the spirit of the thing. The Witches' Aerial Acrobatics team agreed to give a performance of precision flying and write "Magic forever!" in the air with their broomsticks. The magicians supplied twelve dozen doves in appealing pastel shades, to be released after the speeches and toasts.

On the day of the party itself, an extraordinary mixture of magic-makers traipsed along to the wizards' newly built Convention Hall. They all had their best robes on. You've never seen so many sequined stars and spangled symbols in your life.

The first few minutes of the party were taken up with meeting and greeting. Then many of those present began to look about expectantly for something a little more substantial than small talk. They soon found a huge table groaning with goodies and an immense cauldron in which an enticing greenish-blue brew fizzed and spluttered.

Now, neither witches nor wizards are good at forming an orderly line. Magicians are almost as bad. Wizard Wheeze quickly realized that an unseemly free for all would begin if the food, and particularly the brew, were not quickly served.

Unfortunately, he wasn't the only one to have this thought.

"*Ipsle pipsle pup, serve it all up!*" intoned Wizard Wheeze.

"*Six sox sick, dish it out quick!*" yelled Witch Moople.

"*Abracadabradin, let's all dig in!*" chanted two magicians.

"*Take cover!*" hollered Wizard Hoo, who was the first to see what was happening. Hundreds of cakes and pastries hurtled into the air, colliding with each other and showering the assembled company with crumbs. Great globules of bubbling brew also took to the air, threatening to drench the guests diving for shelter under the table.

Wizard Hoo waved his staff to stop the mayhem. Items of food and drink settled back into place.

"Let's try this again," said Wizard Wheeze, "with just one person saying the spell this time." He meant himself, but sadly Witch Moople and the magicians thought he meant *them*. Once again, flying foodstuffs threatened to wipe out the entire party.

When calm had been established once more, a small voice was heard to say, "Excuse me, sir, but why don't we do it the ordinary way?"

Wizard Wheeze looked down at a small elfin boy by his feet. "And what would that be?" he asked.

"You all go and sit down in the next room and we will serve you," said the boy, indicating the team of clearer-uppers.

"But you can't do magic!" protested Wizard Wheeze.

"We don't need to," explained the boy patiently.

The magic-makers trooped off as instructed. Within seconds, the elves had filled plates and cups and made sure that everyone had something to eat and drink.

"Remarkable!" said Wizard Wheeze, with his mouth full of cake.

"How do they do it?" mumbled Witch Moople, already on her fourth beaker of brew.

"A meal without magic! How quaint!" muttered the magicians. "Hey, are those wizards getting all the cake?"

Yes, sometimes too much magic is worse than none at all. If your spelling (I mean the magical kind) still isn't up to scratch, don't worry about it. You may be better off that way!